D1632624

The Little Black Sheep
of Connemara

Elizabeth Shaw was born in Belfast and lived most of her life in Berlin. Winner of the Käthe Kollwitz Prize at the Academy of Art, Berlin, the Leipzig Silver Medal, the Hans Baltzer Prize, and the DDR Art Prize, she wrote and illustrated many books for children. Her internationally acclaimed work is published worldwide in numerous languages.

A beloved classic, *The Little Black Sheep* has found his way to countries such as China, Denmark, Germany, Greece, Japan, Latvia, Mexico, Portugal, Republic of Korea and Sweden.

The Little Black Sheep of Connemara

Elizabeth Shaw

THE O'BRIEN PRESS
DUBLIN

Once there was a shepherd who lived far, far away
in the mountains.

He had a sheepdog called Polo,
who helped him to look after the sheep.

Polo watched the sheep while the shepherd
sat on a mossy rock and knitted.

He knitted socks and scarves and pullovers
and blankets made of pure sheep's wool,
and sold them at the village market.

When the shepherd noticed that a sheep
was straying too far from the flock,
he took out a wooden whistle and blew it.
'Whee!'
This was to tell Polo to run after the sheep
and chase it back to the others.
Polo felt very important then.

At sunset the shepherd blew his whistle again.
'Whee! Whee!'
This meant that Polo should round up the sheep
and chase them into the fold.

As they jumped over the stile, the shepherd
counted them to make sure that all were there.

All the sheep were white except one,
the little black sheep.
When Polo barked 'All to the left!' or 'Right turn!'
or 'Halt!' they *all* did what they were told.

All, that is, except the little black one
who often turned to the left when he should turn
to the right because he was thinking of something else.
This annoyed Polo.

'That black sheep does not do what he is told!'
Polo said to the shepherd. 'And he thinks too much!
Sheep don't need to think. I think for them!'

The little black sheep wished he were like the others.
'Polo sees my mistakes because I'm black,'
he said to the shepherd.

'Could you please knit me a little white jacket
so that I am the same as all the others?'

'Oh no,' said the shepherd, 'you are a very handy little sheep. When I count you all jumping into the fold, I could fall asleep.

But I am always jerked awake by my little black sheep jumping over the stile, especially if you stumble.'

Polo, however, liked all his flock to be just the same.

'You just wait!' he snarled at the black sheep.

'I'll see that you are sold after shearing-time.

Then we'll have a nice tidy flock!'

The little black sheep looked wistfully at the little white fleecy clouds in the sky.

'The shepherd says that they are the souls of good little sheep,' he thought. 'Maybe one day I'll be a little white cloud too!'

Then he noticed that the sky was growing dark behind the mountain.

'It's going to rain!' he called.

'I'll tell you when it's going to rain,' snapped Polo.

Soon after, a sudden storm broke,
with hail and wind and snow.

'My knitting will be ruined!' cried the shepherd.
'Come on, Polo! We must run for shelter.'

They ran to the shepherd's little hut.
'The sheep will be all right.
They have their nice woolly coats.'

The shepherd made a cosy fire to dry his things
and had a hot drink or two.

Night fell.

'We'll see the sheep tomorrow,' said the shepherd.

'No need to worry,' said Polo. 'They'll stay
where they are because I'm not there to tell
them what to do,' and he stretched out beside the fire.

Meanwhile, the sheep were getting nervous
and upset. 'Where is Polo?' they bleated.
'What are we to do?'

'We must look for shelter,' said the little black sheep.
'Follow me! I think I know where there's a cave!'

He led them up the hill to where there were
some hollow rocks with an overhanging ledge.

'We must stay close together and keep
each other warm. I'll look out for the shepherd
when it's light,' said the little black sheep.

The next morning the snow had stopped falling,
but as far as the eye could see all was white.

'Finding sheep today is like trying to find an ice cream
dropped near the North Pole,' said the shepherd.

'I am a bad shepherd,' he sighed,
and he wished he had not slept for so long
the night before. 'Now I've lost my sheep!'

'And how will they manage without me?' said Polo.

Then they saw a black spot on the top of the hill.

'Polo!' cried the shepherd.
'Perhaps that is our little black sheep!'
They hurried towards the black spot.

Under the ledge of rock they found all the sheep,
safe and sound.
There were great celebrations.

'My little black sheep!' said the shepherd fondly,
'but for you I might not have found my flock.'
'Well, maybe he is useful as a landmark, if nothing else,'
growled Polo jealously.

The sun came out and the snow melted.

'Form ranks! Forward march!' barked Polo.

The shepherd carried the little black sheep down the hill.

'I always said you were a handy little sheep,' he said.

When shearing-time came,
the shepherd put the wool into sacks.
There were ten sacks of white wool
and one little sack of black wool.
'Now, how about selling that black sheep?'
said Polo. 'Then we would have a nice
tidy flock.'
'No indeed!' said the shepherd,
'I have a much better idea!'

'I can knit lovely patterns out of black *and* white wool!'
He knitted patterned socks and scarves and blankets,
and sold them for a good price at the market.
With the money he bought some more black sheep.

Soon he had a flock of black, and white,
and spotted sheep.
Each one was different, and that was nice,
because now they were all the same.

First published as *The Little Black Sheep* in 1985 by The O'Brien Press Ltd,
12 Terenure Road East, Rathgar, Dublin 6, D06 HD27, Ireland
Tel: +353 1 4923333; Fax: +353 1 4922777
E-mail: books@obrien.ie
Website: www.obrien.ie
This edition first published 2020
The O'Brien Press is a member of Publishing Ireland.

Copyright for text & illustration © Elizabeth Shaw Estate
Copyright for layout, editing and design © The O'Brien Press Ltd
ISBN: 978-1-78849-179-2

All rights reserved. No part of this book may be reproduced or utilised in any way or by any means, electronic or mechanical, including photocopying, recording or by any information storage and retrieval system without permission in writing from the publisher.

6 5 4 3 2 1
24 23 22 21 20

Printed and bound in Drukarnia Skleniarz, Poland.
The paper in this book is produced using pulp from managed forests.

Published in

DUBLIN
UNESCO
City of Literature